epic! originals

My Pet Slime

Saving Cosmo

epic! originals

My Pet Slime

Saving Cosmo

**Courtney Sheinmel
and Colleen AF Venable**

Illustrated by Renée Kurilla

Andrews McMeel
PUBLISHING®

CAUGHT YOU

The past two days were the weirdest of my life.

They'd ended with me sitting in a cell with my space-traveling Grandma, my old enemy, Claire (who is now my best friend), and my pet slime, of course.

Yes, I have a pet who is made of slime. Cosmo was made out of normal slime, plus paint—I am an artist, after all—but it wasn't until some dust fell on him that he came alive. Well, not just any dust. *Space* dust, and space dust was also the reason we were stuck in that cell. This super evil corporation called MaLa kidnapped Grandma Sadie and demanded the dust back, but they didn't know I had already used it. So we'd had no choice but to save Grandma Sadie ourselves!

We'd had a brilliant plan. Well, maybe we hadn't exactly had a plan, but we had Cosmo, who is not only cute and cuddly, he's also magical!

He flattened into a pancake and snuck under the door at MaLa's headquarters. He picked Grandma Sadie's cell lock! It looked like Cosmo was going to save us all—until we heard a voice behind us yell, "Caught you!"

It was Claire's Uncle Ricky, who worked at MaLa. That's when we knew he must be evil, too!

"Uncle Ricky! What are you doing?" Claire asked. She couldn't believe her uncle was one of the bad guys.

Uncle Ricky looked at us for a second. I could tell he was thinking something through. I could also tell that he hadn't noticed Cosmo.

Finally, Uncle Ricky's face shifted into a smile. He leaned toward Claire and quietly whispered, "Shhh. I have to *pretend* to be on their side, just until I can help you all escape."

Claire looked smug and turned to me and Cosmo. "See, Piper," Claire said. "I told you he wasn't a bad guy. No one in my family could ever be evil!"

I looked over at Grandma Sadie.

She seemed relieved, too.

"Ricky Bryson? Phew! You had me scared for a second there," Grandma Sadie said. "I've always heard such good things about you in the science community. It would be a shame if you had gone bad!"

Uncle Ricky laughed. Like REALLY laughed a bit more than I thought was necessary. It made me nervous.

I looked down at Cosmo. He looked like a normal ball of slime. Cosmo didn't come alive for Uncle Ricky. Did Cosmo know something we didn't? Cosmo also hadn't come alive for my parents, but I'd thought he was just being shy. I wondered why he was being shy now.

"What's the plan, Ricky? I'm so glad to be out of that cell!" Grandma Sadie said.

"I bet you have the *best* plan. Right, Uncle Ricky?" Claire said.

Uncle Ricky looked around, making sure no one could hear. "There's a secret door in Cell 9. It leads to an underground escape tunnel."

"Ugh. Do you have any plans that don't involve me going back into a cell?" Grandma Sadie asked. "I was so bored!"

"You were in Cell 8. Cell 9 is *much* nicer," Uncle Ricky said with a huge smile.

Uncle Ricky started to tiptoe down the hallway, one hand on Claire's head and the other rolling her scooter for her. I walked behind them, my arms wrapped tightly around Cosmo. *Come on, Cosmo! Tell me what to do!* I thought.

We turned a corner and there was a big camera hanging from the ceiling.

"AH YES, PRISONERS, HERE WE ARE! YOU WON'T BE GETTING OUT AGAIN," Uncle Ricky said loudly, his face toward the camera. He turned back and winked at us.

Uncle Ricky unlocked the cell, and I found out he was telling the truth about at least one thing: Cell 9 was definitely nicer than Cell 8. It had a white table, a white sofa, white chairs, and white walls. It was as if someone had dipped the entire room in a can of white paint. Actually, it looked like my dentist's office, only there was no bowl of stickers or giant smiling tooth cartoon on the wall.

It made me wish I had my paint

set. Or better yet, a bunch of paint buckets, like Jackson Pollock used.

Jackson Pollock became famous for his paintings, but he didn't use a brush. Instead, he would throw, splash, and pour his paint. The final works were layers and layers of splatters and swirls, all in different colors. They called it abstract art because it didn't look like anything

other than a whole lot of fun to make.

I looked around the cell and noticed a camera on the wall. There were cameras everywhere here! Uncle Ricky saw me looking at it. He winked—which is a cool grown-up thing I haven't figured out how to do—and he blocked the camera's view with his body.

Uncle Ricky leaned in and whispered, "Okay, see that button on the wall?"

He pointed to a corner of the cell. Sure enough, there was a white button, and around the button you could see the faint outline of a small, square door.

"That button opens a door to

a secret tunnel," Uncle Ricky whispered. "You need to press it for ten seconds, but not yet. Wait for night, when most of the staff has gone home."

"If the staff is home, can't you sneak us out the regular door? That tunnel looks kinda small," I said.

"We can manage! I go through openings that small on the spaceship all the time," said Grandma Sadie.

Have I mentioned that my grandma is the coolest? Because my grandma is the coolest. She's been to space more times than most people have been on a plane!

"There are guards at the exits all night, but the guard in the monitor room always falls asleep after he eats his dinner. The tunnel will be safer, but only if you wait until night," Uncle Ricky said.

"There's no window or clock. How are we going to know when it's night?" I asked.

"NP!" said Claire, looking down at her phone. That means No Problem. But then she looked sad. "Nope, batteries ran out." And then she looked happy again. "Oh! I have an idea. How about you use a secret knock on the door when it's time?"

Claire walked over and knocked on the back of the cell door. Two long taps and three fast taps a little louder: tap...tap...TAP-TAP-TAP.

Uncle Ricky's face fell. "Where did you learn that knock?"

"My dad taught it to me!" Claire beamed.

"My brother and I used that knock for our secret clubhouse when we were kids," Uncle Ricky said, looking down at the floor.

"Great! You already know it!" Claire said.

Uncle Ricky almost looked like he might cry, which was really strange! Then he turned his back to leave.

I looked down and noticed that as Uncle Ricky walked away, Cosmo came back to life.

"Thank you so much, Ricky!" Grandma Sadie said. "I'm glad you're on our side! You're a good guy."

"Yes. Yes, I am," Uncle Ricky said, and he closed the door with a loud CLANK that was followed by a softer *click* as the lock slid into place.

I looked down at Cosmo.

His normal sparkly purple had turned a bright yellow.

2

A SLIME OF A DIFFERENT COLOR

"Cosmo is yellow!" I exclaimed, worried. I held him up for Grandma Sadie and Claire to see.

They both looked at me blankly. Cosmo was back to his normal cute purple color.

"Huh. Well, he *was* yellow," I said,

scratching my head. "I think he was trying to tell us something."

"It's okay, Pipsqueak. It's been a stressful day," Grandma Sadie said.

I sat down on the white floor and hugged Cosmo tight. Grandma Sadie inspected the room while Claire scooted back and forth in the ten feet of space.

"Hmm. Seems like there are actually two cameras in here—one there and one there," Grandma Sadie whispered, tilting her head toward opposite corners of the room. "We'll have to be careful about what we do and what we say until Ricky gives us the signal."

My stomach felt funny. "Are you

sure he's going to help us?" I finally asked.

Claire scoffed. "Of *course* he is! Like my only uncle would keep me in a cell! Ha!"

"I trust Ricky, Piper. And he is Claire's uncle," Grandma Sadie said. "I just wish I'd known he was around earlier so I could have asked for some dominoes to pass the time!"

Less than a minute later we heard a big KA-CHUNG.

Someone was opening the door.

There was no secret knock.

We all huddled together, and I felt Cosmo give me a hug before he turned back into normal slime.

"Hey-ho!" Uncle Ricky said as he

popped his head into the cell. "I thought you might want some things to keep you entertained."

In his hands were more board games than I could count! He put them all down on the white table.

"Yes!" said Claire, inspecting the games. "Checkers, backgammon, a bag of marbles, Monopoly, Pictionary, and a jigsaw puzzle of a cute cat!"

"And these are for you, Sadie," Uncle Ricky said, handing Grandma a brand-new box of dominoes.

"That's so sweet of you, Ricky!" Grandma

Sadie said, taking the dominoes with a big smile. "I meant to ask before—have you seen Eric? He was helping me, but I haven't seen him in a while."

"Oh yeah, Eric," Uncle Ricky said. "He, uh, went on break."

In my hands I felt Cosmo come alive. I looked down, and he was bright yellow again! This time, Grandma Sadie noticed. I could see it in her eyes, but she didn't say anything.

"I have one more surprise," Uncle Ricky said. He ducked through the door, and when he came back, he was holding a tray. On the tray were glasses of milk and fresh brownies! They smelled delicious.

In my hands, Cosmo turned back to purple. Maybe Uncle Ricky wasn't a bad guy after all.

"See?" Claire whispered, her mouth full of brownie. "I told you my uncle was a good guy. Piper was worried you weren't really trying to save us!"

"Of course I am," Uncle Ricky whispered back.

Grandma Sadie looked me straight in the eyes, and then flicked her eyes down toward my hands. When I looked down at Cosmo, I saw he was yellow again.

"Bye, Uncle Ricky!" Claire said as he started to close the door. "Don't forget our secret knock," she added in a whisper.

"Couldn't if I tried," Uncle Ricky said as the door clanked shut.

As soon as he was gone, Grandma Sadie held her hands in front of her mouth so the people watching the cameras couldn't see her speaking.

"Girls," she whispered. "I think we're in trouble."

3

COSMO'S NEW POWER

Grandma Sadie bent down and put her face right next to Cosmo. "Hi, Cosmo. I love soda," she said.

That made me laugh. "No you don't! You always say it tickles your nose, and it's super bad for you anyway—"

I stopped my sentence short. Cosmo had turned yellow.

"Whoa! You were right. He's yellow! I hope he's not sick," Claire said, feeling his little forehead to see if he had a fever.

"I think we just discovered another one of Cosmo's powers," said Grandma Sadie.

"Huh?" Claire said.

"Say something that's true, Claire. How about you tell me how much you like your scooter," Grandma Sadie said.

"I love my scooter! It's the best scooter! It's really fast even without Cosmo supercharging—whoa!" Claire cut herself off.

Cosmo had turned back to purple.

"I think he can tell when someone is lying," I said.

"What? That's not possible!" Claire said.

"I'll try it. Um...I don't like making art at all," I lied.

Cosmo turned yellow.

"Now say something true," Grandma Sadie said.

"I want to be a professional artist when I grow up!" I said.

Cosmo's slime returned to its usual sparkly purple.

"That's so cool!" Claire exclaimed.

"But remember the first time he turned yellow?" I asked.

Grandma Sadie nodded and gave me a hug. "I do, Pipsqueak. I do."

Claire put another brownie in her

mouth. "You lost me there," she said between chews.

"It was when your uncle said he was going to help us," I said. "I think he may be lying."

I felt bad making Claire sad. She was my best friend. After Cosmo and Grandma Sadie, of course. She stopped chewing and her face got red.

"That's not true. No one in my family would be that awful," Claire said, looking away. "You'll see when that door opens!"

Claire pointed toward the secret button her uncle had told us about. I could tell the gears were turning in her head. She ran over to the wall and pressed it. We all waited.

One...two...three...four...

Claire counted all the way to fifteen. Nothing happened. There was no secret door. Uncle Ricky had definitely lied.

Cosmo reached out to Claire. I handed him to her, and he hugged her. She buried her face in his squishy body. "We're going to be stuck here forever," she said.

"It's okay, Claire. We'll get out of this! Cosmo will flatten himself down and sneak under the door again!

Then he'll pick the lock! You'll be safe at home in no time, and then we can tell the police what MaLa has been up to."

Right then a voice came over a speaker and we all jumped in surprise. It was a voice we all knew.

"Ugh! Settle down, Claire. I'm not one of the bad guys. Not really." Uncle Ricky's voice was distorted by the speakers, but it was definitely

him. And he was definitely one of the bad guys.

"You were never supposed to get mixed up in this!" Uncle Ricky continued. "This isn't about you. It's about the space dust. If your friend would just hand it over..."

Then Uncle Ricky's voice was interrupted by another voice I recognized—a much scarier one.

It was the triangle-hair lady— Doreen. She was the first scary MaLa employee I had encountered, and what she said made me shake in my shoes.

"That slime... I just saw it move! It's alive! It must have absorbed the space dust. Go get it!"

30

4

THE OTHER PRISONER

"Quick, Cosmo, we need to get out of here!" I yelled, frantically grabbing him from Claire's arms.

But the MaLa employees were too fast.

The second the door opened, Cosmo turned back into a normal

blob, losing all his powers. I held on to him as tight as I could.

But there were too many of them. Two of them grabbed Grandma Sadie. Uncle Ricky picked up Claire. Someone grabbed me. I saw hands reaching for Cosmo, but I couldn't let go! I had to be strong! I had to...

I felt Cosmo slip from my fingers. NO!

"Got it, Doreen!" a man with a long, gray goatee yelled at Doreen.

He examined Cosmo and made a weird face. "Whatever *it* is. Gross."

It was over before I had a chance to react.

The door closed with a CLANK! Cosmo was gone.

I started to cry.

Claire pounded on the door and yelled, "HOW DARE YOU! AND YOU CALL YOURSELVES SCIENTISTS!"

Then I heard it: a faint voice from the wall. It sounded like it was coming from another cell.

"Grandma! I think there's someone in the next cell," I said.

"I heard it, too. ERIC, IS THAT YOU?" she yelled directly at the wall.

There was a reply, but it was too soft to hear.

Grandma Sadie ran to the table and picked up two glasses of milk. She held them out to Claire and me.

"Quick! Drink these," Grandma Sadie said.

"Yeah! Those meanies think they can steal Cosmo *and* my scooter? We're going to drink this milk and . . . get super buff and break out of here?" Claire said, then drank her milk in a single gulp.

I just held mine while Grandma Sadie grabbed the third glass and drank it quickly. "I don't understand," I said, slowly wiping away my tears.

"Done!" Claire said.

Grandma Sadie placed the open end of her empty glass against the wall and put her ear against the bottom of the glass.

"Uh, what are you doing?" asked Claire.

"A glass can help amplify a sound. When I press my ear against it, the sound seems louder and is easier to understand," Grandma Sadie explained.

"Whoa, cool. I want to try, too!" Claire put her glass against the wall and leaned in to listen.

I was too sad to drink milk or eat brownies or do anything ever again. I had lost Cosmo.

"ERIC! IS THAT YOU?"

Grandma Sadie yelled at the wall.

I heard a muffled voice.

"OH NO! ARE YOU BEING PUNISHED FOR HELPING ME?" Grandma Sadie yelled back.

There was some more muffled speaking.

"YES, THEY TOOK MY GRANDDAUGHTER'S PET, COSMO—"

"AND MY SCOOTER!" interrupted Claire.

It was weird to hear only one side of the conversation, but my heart was too broken to care. That is, until Grandma said something that got my attention.

"YOU KNOW WHERE THEY TOOK COSMO?"

Cosmo! I drank my milk quickly and put my glass against the wall.

"They have a special lab where they test anything related to space dust. It's Lab Q. It's on the second floor, near the racquetball courts," Eric said. His voice was faint, but it was clear enough to understand.

"They have racquetball courts? Weird," said Claire.

My mind started racing. We had to get to the second floor! I was developing A PLAN!

I grabbed a $100 bill from the Monopoly box and started to fold it.

Grandma Sadie noticed. "You okay, Pipsqueak?" she asked.

"More than okay! I have a plan!" I replied.

5

GET OUT OF JAIL FREE

I've always been really good at origami. I can remember how to make a lot of things by heart! Here are some things I can make without any instructions at all:

41

1. **A crane**
2. **A frog**
3. **A paper cup**

The cup was the one that was going to save us. I folded the monopoly money as quickly as I could.

"An origami paper cup? We already have cups," Claire said, holding up her empty milk glass.

"These aren't for milk," I said.

I made my last fold and popped open the top of the cup.

Perfect!

I made a second one and

then motioned for Claire and Grandma to lean in, and I quietly told them my plan.

Grandma Sadie smiled. I could tell she was proud.

"Brilliant, Pipsqueak!" she whispered.

"Okay, are you ready?" I asked.

Claire nodded and Grandma gave a thumbs-up as she sat down on the couch.

I stood on the couch and put my legs over Grandma's shoulders. When she stood up, I felt like the tallest person in the world!

Well, maybe not the tallest in the WORLD, but definitely tall enough to reach the cameras.

I took one of my origami cups and placed it over the lens of one camera. It was a near-perfect fit!

"Wow, cool!" Claire said from the ground. "When we get out of here, can you teach me how to make those?"

"Definitely!" I said, proud of myself.

I quickly covered the second camera, and then Grandma Sadie set me down.

"Okay, kids—hurry! We don't know how long it'll be before they notice that they can't see us anymore. But we'll be ready," Grandma Sadie whispered.

We got to work, keeping our voices low so they wouldn't hear our plan. It took about five minutes before we heard fast footsteps coming down the hall.

We crouched near the door. When the lock clicked, Doreen, Uncle Ricky, and the other MaLa bad guys who had taken Cosmo all rushed into the room.

"What is...ACK!" Doreen didn't get a chance to finish her sentence because she fell, slipping on the marbles we had spilled all over the floor by the door. The other MaLa employees tripped and landed right on top of her.

Our plan had worked!

"Go, go, go!" Grandma Sadie said as we ran out of the open door, careful to avoid the marbles.

"Hey! No!" Uncle Ricky cried as we pulled the door closed.

It shut with a CLANK and a click. Those were the best sounds I had ever heard.

"Let's go get Cosmo!" I said.

"I have to do one thing first," Claire said.

She walked up to the door and raised a fist.

Tap...tap...TAP-TAP-TAP.

It was the secret knock her dad had taught her—the one he had used with Uncle Ricky when they were kids.

"You don't get to use the knock anymore, Uncle Ricky! I'm telling my dad what you did!"

Claire turned back. "We can go now," she said. She looked sadder than I had ever seen her.

Grandma Sadie yelled at the door to Cell 7. "HOLD TIGHT, ERIC! WE'LL GET YOU OUT!"

"Follow me," Grandma Sadie said.

We ran down the long hallway.

The dark hallway's walls were

plain and gray. I thought about how perfect they'd be for Banksy, an English artist who likes to draw on random streets, bridges, and walls when no one is looking.

Drawing on random things that don't belong to you sounds like something you shouldn't do, but no one minds it when Banksy does it. Their art is really valuable. Spotting something new by Banksy is a really big deal.

Actually, Banksy isn't even their real name. No one knows Banksy's real name. Lots of people have tried to figure it out, but it's still a mystery.

We reached the stairs and rushed up them. "There's the racquetball courts," I said, pointing to a big set of glass windows and forgetting all about Banksy.

"Someone left a ball in the hallway," Claire said, holding up a dark blue rubber ball.

Grandma crouched down by the door next to the courts. "Then that must be the lab they have Cosmo in. Be careful. There may be more MaLa employees around."

I stood up and looked into the lab's tiny glass window.

There was Cosmo!

But he looked different. He wasn't purple or even yellow.

He was green.

Suddenly he turned back to

normal slime, and I knew someone else must be in the room with him. The MaLa employee with the long, gray goatee sat down at a computer near Cosmo. He had his lunch bag open and was typing away with one hand while holding a sad-looking sandwich with the other. His back was to the door, and I noticed his key card on the desk.

"It's just one guy, and I see his key card," I said.

We could hear the lab guy talking to himself through the door.

"I don't know what Doreen thought she saw," he muttered. "This blob is definitely not alive."

"How do we get Cosmo out of there?" Claire whispered.

I reached into my pockets and pulled out a bunch of the dominoes Uncle Ricky had given Grandma Sadie earlier.

"With these!" I said.

"I have a feeling you have another plan, Pipsqueak," Grandma Sadie said softly.

I did indeed.

6

BOWLING FOR SLIME

It took us a few minutes to set up the dominoes.

Claire held the racquetball tight to her chest.

"You ready?" I asked her.

"My mom and I go bowling all the time. I'm ready!" she said.

We crept past the door to the lab

53

and down to the end of the hallway. Then we hid just around the corner.

Claire held the ball like a professional bowler. She took a deep breath and rolled.

The ball sped down the hallway in a perfectly straight line. It was headed RIGHT toward the first domino—or so we thought.

It missed by less than an inch.

"Oh no!" Claire cried, then covered her mouth.

"Don't get upset quite yet," Grandma Sadie whispered with a smile.

Because here's the thing about rubber balls: they bounce. And Grandma Sadie knew all about physics and angles.

It was actually a perfect shot. The ball hit the wall and ricocheted twice, knocking over the first domino and setting off the chain reaction.

I knew it was going to be loud, but I hadn't realized HOW loud. The dominoes started falling in the hallway and then wound into the stairwell and down the stairs.

Clack...clack...clack...CLACK-CLACK-CLACK-CLACK they went.

The MaLa lab employee opened the door, muttering, "What on earth is that noise?" as he walked down the stairs to investigate.

While his back was turned, we rushed into the lab.

Cosmo came back to life and smiled, but he didn't look quite right. His eyes looked sad.

"Cosmo, are you okay, boy?" I asked, my heart filled with worry.

"Cosmo is green! What does that mean? Was someone lying again?" Claire asked.

"I'm afraid that's not it," Grandma Sadie said. "I think Cosmo may be sick."

I started to hug him tight.

"Be careful, Pipsqueak. You don't want to hurt him even more. This lunch bag looks soft enough to protect him," Grandma Sadie said. She dumped the rest of goatee guy's lunch onto the floor and gently put Cosmo in the bag. Then she grabbed the key card off the desk.

While the goatee guy was still on

the stairs, we took the elevator back down to the cells. I could hear Doreen yelling at her staff in Cell 9. If I hadn't been so worried about Cosmo, I probably would have laughed.

Grandma ran to Cell 7 and put the card against the door. We heard a click, and the door opened.

"Eric!" Grandma Sadie hugged the man who came out of the cell. "This is Eric, girls. He's the MaLa employee who helped me."

"Pretty sure that's *former* employee," Eric said with a laugh.

"No time for introductions! Let's get out of here!" I said and started for the exit.

"No! Not that way. It's not safe," Eric said. "I know another way."

Eric walked to a spot on the floor. He put his hand on the wall and slid a tile aside. Underneath it was a secret button—a real one, this time.

A trapdoor opened in the floor.

"This way," Eric said.

Then he jumped through the hole in the floor.

I wondered if we should trust Eric. What if he was like Uncle Ricky and was just trying to trick us?

I looked into the lunch bag, hoping Cosmo would give me a hint, but his eyes were barely open and he still looked more green than anything.

Grandma Sadie jumped in.

Then Claire jumped in.

What should I do? I rested my head on the bag that held Cosmo.

I had to be brave.

So I jumped.

7

THE PLASTIC CHARIOT

WHOOSH!

It was a slide!

Down I went. Down the longest, darkest, most twisty slide I'd ever been on. It was super scary.

Maybe if this had been a slide at an amusement park, it would've been the fun kind of scary. But since it was

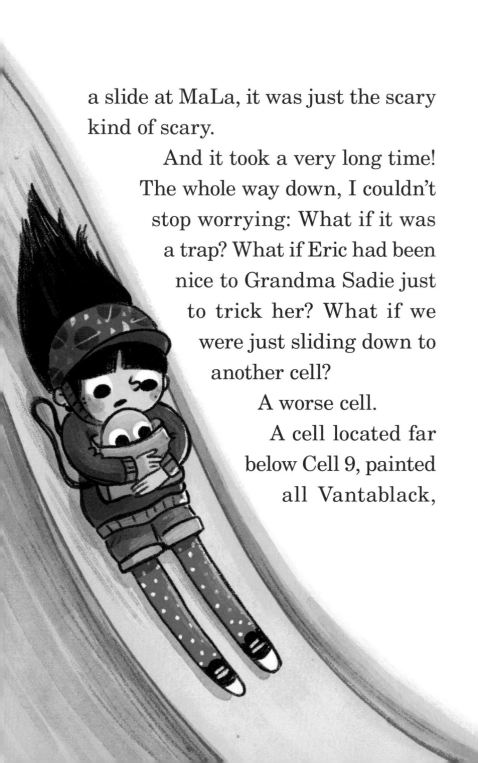

a slide at MaLa, it was just the scary kind of scary.

And it took a very long time! The whole way down, I couldn't stop worrying: What if it was a trap? What if Eric had been nice to Grandma Sadie just to trick her? What if we were just sliding down to another cell?

A worse cell.

A cell located far below Cell 9, painted all Vantablack,

the blackest black there is, instead of all white.

What if we never saw the light of day again?

I twisted down one last curve and the slide spit me out in a plop, right on top of Claire.

"Ow!" she said.

"Sorry," I told her. I rolled out of the way and dusted myself off. I peeked into the bag. Cosmo had come back to life but was still light green. "You okay, boy?" I asked him.

He gurgled.

"Everyone all right?" Grandma Sadie asked.

"Yeah, I guess," I said.

"Now up those stairs!" Eric said.

Claire started to follow him, but I grabbed her arm and stopped her.

"What's the matter?" she asked.

"It could be a trap," I whispered. "What if Eric is like Uncle Ricky?"

Claire's eyes widened. "A trap?!" she practically screamed.

"WAM," Claire said to Eric. He stopped and looked back.

"Huh?" he asked.

"Wait. A. Minute," Claire said. "Why should we—"

"Well, I'll be," Eric said. "That slime in your arms just blinked."

Cosmo had popped his head out of the bag.

My heart soared! Eric WAS a good guy!

"This is Cosmo," I said. "He's my pet. He doesn't come alive for just anyone. It's just Grandma Sadie, Claire, me, and now you, too!"

"Amazing! Once we're all safe, I want to hear all about him," Eric said.

"Okay," I said. I turned to Claire. "Cosmo trusts Eric. I think we can, too."

The four of us—plus Cosmo—raced up the stairs. But it's hard to race up so many flights. After a while, you start to slow down and huff and puff. About halfway through I had to stop and catch my breath. We got to the top and Eric pushed open a heavy metal door. I had to squint because the sun was so strong.

The sun!

That could only mean one thing.

"Hooray, we're outside!" I cheered. We were standing in a parking lot outside the building.

Claire twirled around. "I missed you, sunshine," she said. "I missed you, fresh air. I missed you, sidewalks and buildings and street signs."

"You can say hi to the street signs later. We have to keep moving!" Grandma Sadie said, walking quickly.

"Where do we go now? MaLa knows where I live, and Uncle Ricky knows where Claire lives," I said.

Claire shook her head sadly. "You think you know the members of your own family. But I don't know Uncle Ricky at all."

I patted Claire's shoulder.

Grandma Sadie took a deep breath. "There's only one place to go," she said. "My lab."

"You have a lab?" I asked. "I didn't know that."

"No one knows," Grandma Sadie said. "Not even your mom. Not even my colleagues at AstroBlast. It's kinda like Batman's cave—a secret that I've kept hidden for years."

"Whoa," Claire said.

Whoa was right. I guess Claire wasn't the only person who didn't know a member of her own family as well as she thought she did.

"Okay!" Eric said, stopping. "The bus should be here any minute!"

"The bus?!" Claire exclaimed.

"Oh dear, I can't imagine Doreen will tolerate being locked up long enough for that," said Grandma Sadie.

"If only we had a scooter," I said.

"Uncle Ricky totally owes me another scooter," Claire grumbled as we followed Eric around the corner.

"I'm so sorry, Claire," Grandma Sadie said. "I understand it's sad to lose your favorite scooter."

"You scoot?" Claire asked her.

"With the best!" Grandma Sadie said.

"THERE THEY ARE!" came a shout from a window of the MaLa building. Doreen and Uncle Ricky had gotten out.

"What are we going to do?" Claire asked nervously.

I looked around. I saw an overturned orange shopping cart, a bunch of messy fast-food wrappers, a mostly used roll of duct tape, and a pair of smelly work boots.

Gross! People need to clean up after themselves better! Also, who goes home without their shoes? But then I got an idea! I looked at Cosmo. He was still green, but he seemed to know exactly what I was thinking.

"Do you think you can do it, boy?"

He nodded his little head and smiled for the first time since we'd rescued him from the lab.

"Quick, Claire! Take the laces

out of those boots!" I said.

"Ew. No thank you," Claire said, holding her nose. But then she looked at me and realized I was serious. Like a good friend, she sighed and started to unlace the boots.

"Grandma Sadie, Eric, help me pick up this cart!" I said.

"You got it, Pipsqueak! I have a feeling you've cooked up a plan in that brilliant brain of yours," Grandma Sadie replied as we lifted the cart back onto its wheels.

Claire handed me the shoelaces. I grabbed the duct tape and taped one of the laces to the front left wheel and the other to the front right wheel.

"Everybody in!" I yelled.

Grandma Sadie jumped into the cart and helped Claire and me get in. We buckled our helmets quickly.

"Doesn't someone need to stay outside to push?" Eric asked.

The MaLa crew was running out the front door of the building.

"Cosmo will do it! Get in!" I yelled.

The moment Eric swung his second leg into the cart, I whispered to Cosmo and hugged him very, very gently. "I know you're feeling sick, but please try! You've got this, Cosmo."

With that, Cosmo activated his superpowers and we were off! Eric nearly fell over. The cart flew out of the parking lot faster than I ever thought a cart could go.

I pulled on the left shoelace, and the cart turned left. I pulled on the right lace, and the cart turned right.

It was working! I steered us toward the sidewalk.

"Is Cosmo doing that?" Grandma Sadie asked.

"Yup!" I replied proudly.

"Well aren't you full of surprises," she said, smiling at him.

Behind us, Uncle Ricky and Doreen had gotten into a car.

"Faster!" Claire cried.

"I don't think we can go any faster," Eric said.

"But they're gaining on us!" she said.

I was afraid to look, but I couldn't help myself. I turned around. Uncle Ricky was hanging out the passenger-side window. We were done for.

Or so I thought. I was so scared that I closed my eyes and hugged Cosmo really tight.

"Go, Cosmo!" Claire yelled.

The shopping cart was going faster and faster. I twisted around, watching as Uncle Ricky became a smaller and smaller dot behind us until we couldn't see him at all anymore.

"We did it!" Grandma Sadie said, throwing her arms up in the air as if we were on a roller coaster.

We had escaped. For now.

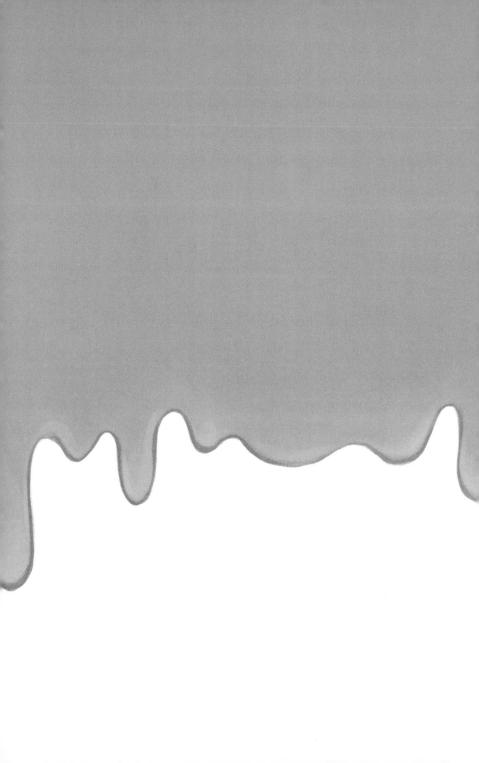

8

GRANDMA SADIE'S SECRET SCIENCE LAB

We didn't slow down until we got to Grandma Sadie's house.

"I'm sure the MaLa folks will be snooping around here before long," Grandma Sadie said. "We need to hide the cart. Piper, will you and Claire get the tarp from the shed?"

"We're on it," I said. I knew I'd need both hands, so I put Cosmo down on a lawn chair. He still looked frail and light green. "I'll be right back," I told him.

Claire followed me as I jogged around the side of the house to Grandma Sadie's backyard. I weaved through Grandma Sadie's collection of garden gnomes.

"There must be a hundred of these ugly things," Claire said.

"Thirty-four," I told her. "And I think they're cute."

"I've almost tripped three times," Claire said. "That's the opposite of cute to me."

I pulled open the shed door.

"Look, there's the tarp," I said.

Claire and I lugged it back over to the garage, being careful not to trip over any gnomes. Grandma Sadie and Eric helped us cover the shopping cart.

I scooped up Cosmo and gave him a quick hug. "Good job waiting for me. We'll get you healthy in no time," I told him.

"Where's the secret lab?" Claire asked.

"I'll show you," Grandma Sadie

said. We walked to the backyard. Grandma bent down and pulled off her left shoe.

"You want us to take our shoes off before we go inside?" Eric asked.

"My parents have the same rule," Claire said. "But can we at least wait until we're *inside* the front door? I don't want my socks to get dirty."

"Everyone can keep their shoes on," Grandma Sadie said.

She pulled up the insole of her shoe, and then she pulled out a tiny brass key.

Grandma Sadie slipped her shoe back on and walked over to the steps by the back door. But she didn't go up the steps.

She bent down next to the garden gnome that sat beside the bottom step, and she tipped back its little red hat.

"I didn't know their hats came off like that," I said.

"They usually don't," Grandma Sadie said. "This one is special."

Underneath the hat was a small keyhole. Grandma Sadie inserted the key she'd taken out of her shoe, and the steps flipped backward and turned into a stairwell that led underneath the house.

"Well, I'll be," Eric said.

I was speechless. Claire's mouth was hanging open, but she didn't say anything, either.

Grandma Sadie jogged down the steps, and the rest of us followed.

When we got to the bottom, the stairs flipped back up so they were flush with the ceiling.

I set Cosmo down on a chair and looked around the room. Cosmo gurgled up at me.

"Will he be safe here?" I asked Grandma Sadie.

"We're all safe down here," Grandma said. "You can't see a trace of this room from the backyard. You can't even hear any noise from it.

Everything is soundproof."

"Whoa," Claire said.

She stepped deeper into the room, and so did I. There were velvety overstuffed chairs and a big wooden desk piled high with papers. On the far side of the room, there was a lab table covered with beakers full of different substances. A pink one was bubbling like a brook. A blue one was as still as a lake. An orange one was steaming like a geyser. And a green one was swishing back and forth, like ocean waves.

"First, let's get Cosmo some food!" Grandma Sadie said. "When's the last time he ate? Maybe he's just hungry."

"I can sneak upstairs and get something to eat," Eric offered.

"No need," Grandma Sadie told him. "We have everything we need right down here."

She opened up a small fridge and pulled out meat and cheese and hamburger buns.

"But how will we cook it?" I asked. "I don't see a stove."

"We don't need one," Grandma Sadie said.

For a second, I was worried she was planning to serve us raw meat, which is not safe for anyone to eat— even pets made of slime.

"Bunsen burners!" she said.

Grandma turned a few handles

and used a metal tool that made sparks to light a metal tube standing on her lab table. The flame was smaller than the kind on a stove, but it was bigger than a candle's flame. Grandma set up a metal rack over it and put a pan on top. Within minutes, the burgers were sizzling in the pan.

"Who wants cheese?" Grandma Sadie asked.

"Meeeeeee!" Claire said.

"You got it," Grandma said. "Eric?"

"I wish I could," Eric said, "but I'm allergic to dairy."

I gave him a sad smile. I know what it's like to have allergies. I can't be around any cute and furry pets because I'm allergic to them. That's why I'm so lucky to have Cosmo.

While she made our food, Grandma also made a tiny version of her Bunsen burgers just for Cosmo.

"There you go, boy. Eat up," I said, setting his burger in front of him.

"What are all these photos on your wall?" Claire asked.

"Just a few things that inspire me," she said. "Come over here, Pipsqueak. I want you to see my gallery."

Grandma Sadie swept an arm toward a wall decorated with framed photos. "This is Albert Einstein, who came up with the world's most famous equation," Grandma Sadie said. "Energy equals the mass of an object times the speed of light squared."

"What does that mean?" I asked.

"It means no matter how small an object is, it contains a tremendous amount of energy," she told me.

"Like Cosmo," I said.

"Sort of." She moved to the next picture. "And here's Galileo Galilei. He was a scientist and an astronomer who helped develop the scientific method."

"This is Sally Ride," Grandma Sadie went on. "She was a physicist and an astronaut and the first American woman in space. And this is Isaac Newton. He came up with the law of motion that says for every action there's an equal and opposite reaction. And over here we have—"

"Leonardo da Vinci!" I said. "He was one of the most famous artists in the world. He painted the *Mona Lisa,* the *Last Supper,* and a lot of other things. Why do you have a picture of an artist in your lab?"

"He's most famous for his artwork," Grandma Sadie said. "But people aren't just one thing. Da Vinci sure wasn't! Besides being an artist, he was also an engineer, an inventor, an architect, a botanist, a musician, a writer, a mathematician...and a scientist."

"Wow," I said. "What about all these pictures of Mom, Dad, and me?" I asked. "I know we're a lot of things, too. But we're not scientists."

"Maybe not," Grandma Sadie said, "but you three are my greatest inspirations." She gave me a squeeze.

THE RINGS OF JUPITER

Cosmo hadn't even touched the burger, and he was still a light shade of green. This was a bad sign.

"If he's not hungry, what could be wrong with him?" I asked.

"I'm not sure yet, Pipsqueak," Grandma Sadie said. "I'll get my

93

stethoscope and check him out."

"Why do you have a stethoscope?" Claire asked. "You're not a doctor."

"Stethoscopes listen to internal sounds," Grandma Sadie explained. "Sometimes I encounter things in space that—"

"Aliens?" Claire interrupted.

Grandma Sadie gave a little smile. "I've found the stethoscope to be a very helpful tool," she said. She pulled one out of a drawer and scooted closer to Cosmo. His little green body started to tremble.

"Don't worry, it won't hurt," I told him. "It won't, will it, Grandma?"

"Of course not," she said.

She warmed up the flat part of

the stethoscope, which is called the bell, with her palm, just like they do at the doctor's office. Then she put it on Cosmo's little body—first his front, then his back, his sides, the top of his head, and his belly.

"Is he okay?" I asked anxiously.

"Hold on, Pipsqueak," Grandma Sadie said. "I still need to take some measurements."

I paced nervously as Grandma continued her examination.

"Hey," Eric said. "Why don't you tell me more about Cosmo?"

I could tell he was trying to distract me and cheer me up.

"I made him out of slime," I said. "I used my regular slime recipe, which is glue, baking soda, and my mom's contact lens solution. Plus, I used red and blue food coloring because they make purple, and purple is my favorite color."

"And then he just came to life?" Eric asked.

"Not exactly," I said. I looked over at Grandma Sadie to see if I should say the next part. She nodded.

"Grandma Sadie gave me a bottle of space dust," I said. "At first it

looked just like regular old Earth dust. But when I woke up in the middle of the night, I noticed it was glowing. When I opened the bottle, the dust flew out and landed on Cosmo. That's when he came to life."

"Incredible. Just incredible," Eric said. "I'd heard there was space dust with magical powers floating in the cosmos. But I didn't know anyone had actually found it."

"Of course, it's not actually *magical*," Grandma said.

"That's right," Eric agreed. "Lots of things seem like magic before we understand them, and I'm sure someday we'll understand what makes space dust act like it does.

But even then, it'll still seem pretty amazing."

"To be honest, I didn't even believe that space dust existed," Grandma Sadie said. "Of course, I'd also heard rumors about it. But I figured it was just a myth, like the one about the moon being made of cheese."

"The moon is made of cheese?" I asked.

"No, of course not," Eric said. "If it were, I'd be allergic to it. But I've been to the moon eleven times, and I've never even had an upset stomach there. Anyway, back to the space dust..."

"Right," Grandma Sadie said. "I'd

gone on a mission to Jupiter to collect specimens from the rings."

"Saturn is the planet with rings," Claire said.

"Saturn does have rings," Grandma Sadie agreed. "But so do Uranus, Neptune, and Jupiter. Jupiter's three rings are made up mostly of dust. And right there, in the center of the middle ring, I noticed that the dust was shimmering a little differently. And I thought maybe, just maybe, the rumors were true."

"It was hiding in plain sight," Eric said.

"So to speak," Grandma Sadie said. "I collected the specimen and brought it back to Earth. At that point, I didn't know what powers the dust would have." She gave Cosmo's head a pat. "My guess is we haven't seen all it can do."

"You hear that, boy?" I asked. "You probably have even more powers!"

Cosmo smiled weakly.

"When you have something with untapped power, you want to keep it somewhere very safe," Grandma Sadie said. "That's why I gave the dust to Piper."

"That doesn't make sense," Claire said. "No offense, but Piper is just a kid."

"I know," Grandma Sadie said. "And I'm sorry, Pipsqueak."

"What are you sorry for?" I asked.

"I thought the dust would be safe with you and would just be a neat souvenir from space. I had no idea having it would jeopardize your safety." Grandma Sadie shook her head sadly. I didn't know what to say.

Grandma set down her stethoscope. "Well, he sounds all right, but there's still something off. Let me get my scale."

"Hey," Eric said, trying to cheer me up again. "Is anyone in the mood for dessert? I saw some astronaut ice cream on the shelf over there."

Here are some things to know about astronaut ice cream:

101

1. It's freeze-dried, which means the water has been sucked out of it.
2. It's thicker and stickier than regular ice cream.
3. It's not as good as regular ice cream, but it's still tasty.

The reason I know these astronaut ice cream facts is that Grandma Sadie brought some back for me to taste four space trips ago.

"I'll have some," Claire said.

"What about you, Sadie?" Eric asked.

"Let's try giving my share to Cosmo," Grandma Sadie said.

Eric tore open a package of astronaut ice cream and broke it into parts. It breaks like stale bread but actually melts once you put it in your mouth.

"Want a taste, Cosmo?" I asked.

I held out a piece of chocolate astronaut ice cream. Cosmo sniffed it. Then he shook his head.

"I don't understand something about this whole 'magical space dust' thing," Claire said. "Why is Cosmo alive for us, but not for other people?"

"I think Cosmo is becoming less shy, but he still only comes alive for people he thinks are safe," I said. "Right, Grandma Sadie?"

"It's the best explanation I've come up with," Grandma said. "Cosmo is a great judge of character."

"But...," Claire said.

"But what?" I asked.

"Well, the truth is, I wasn't always kind to you, Piper. I went into your backpack without asking, and then I lied about it."

"Yeah, you did," I said. "But I forgave you."

"Still, that wasn't kind," Claire said. "And that was the same day Cosmo turned alive for me."

"Look at what you've done for Piper *today*," Grandma Sadie said. "And for me. And for Cosmo."

"Seems to me that Cosmo always knew you had it in you," I said.

Claire smiled quietly, looking at her feet.

Grandma Sadie carried Cosmo over to a table covered in beakers.

"Piper, Claire—can you clear these off so I have some room to work?" she asked.

We nodded. Claire picked up the beaker with the blue stuff in it. I picked up the one with the pink stuff.

"Careful," Grandma Sadie warned.

Cosmo gave an anxious gurgle.

"I didn't mean to scare you," Grandma Sadie told him. "I just need to run a few more tests."

She placed him on a scale. Numbers popped up. "Hmmm," she said.

Grandma Sadie stuck tiny little stickers to Cosmo, and then connected

the stickers to wires. She looked at a black screen with a bunch of lines and green words on it.

"What are you getting?" Eric asked.

"Sixteen over eleven," Grandma Sadie said. "Fourteen and nine."

"Oh," Eric said.

I did not like the way it sounded when he said *oh*.

"What's wrong?" I asked.

"Cosmo's measurements aren't adding up," Grandma Sadie said.

"Is that bad?"

She didn't answer.

I knew what no answer meant: it was bad. Maybe it was even very bad.

"Could it be the difference in gravity?" Eric asked.

"What about gravity?" I asked.

"Jupiter's gravity is 2.4 times the Earth's," Grandma Sadie said.

"I don't understand," I said.

"Me either," Claire said.

"You're about two and a half times heavier there than you are on Earth," Grandma Sadie explained. "It's affecting Cosmo and making him sick."

"So...what if we dressed Cosmo in some really heavy clothes?" I asked. "My snowsuit is heavy. So are my winter boots."

"I wish it were that easy," Grandma Sadie said. "The clothes might change the numbers on the scale, but Cosmo's core weight would still be lighter than it should be."

"He didn't eat very much today," Claire said. "That could affect his weight."

"Oh yeah!" I said. "He didn't touch his burger or the ice cream. Maybe he just needs to eat more. I know he loves Oreos. He ate every single one in my lunch the other day. Do you have any down here?"

"I don't," Grandma Sadie said. "But Cosmo's lack of hunger is a symptom, not the problem."

"Huh?"

"The reason he's not eating is because his numbers are off, not the other way around," Grandma Sadie said.

"So what can we do?" I asked.

"I think there's only one thing to do," Eric said.

"Yes. It looks that way," Grandma Sadie said.

"What?" I asked. "What's the one thing? Whatever it is, we'll do it."

Grandma Sadie didn't answer.

"What?" I said, louder this time.

"We have to send Cosmo to live on Jupiter," she said.

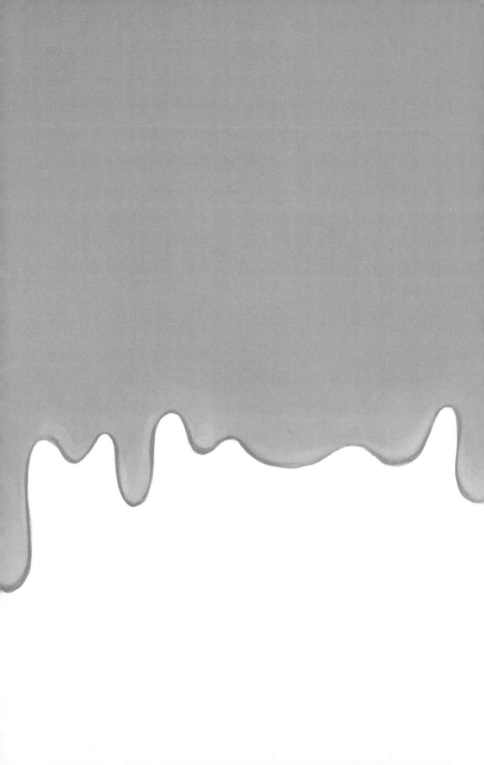

10

T-MINUS TOO-LITTLE-TIME TO LIFTOFF

"No, no, no," I said, pulling Cosmo close to me. "Not Jupiter! Anything but Jupiter!"

"I'm really sorry, and I wish there were another way," Eric said.

I lifted my head from Cosmo's soft, squishy neck. "But...but..."

"Don't squeeze him too tight right now, Pipsqueak," Grandma Sadie said. "He's very sensitive at the moment. The space dust came from Jupiter. Sadly, he belongs there, not on Earth."

"Oh, I'm so sorry, Cosmo," I said, and I loosened my grip. "I don't want to make things worse for you. It's just so hard. I want to hug you and hold you forever!"

"I know, Piper. I know," said

Grandma Sadie. "I feel awful about it. But this is the best way I know to give Cosmo a chance to recover."

"At least if he goes to Jupiter he'll be safe from everyone at MaLa," Claire said. She patted my arm.

I knew she was trying to be nice. But when you're really sad, there's no "at least" that can make things better.

"How will we get him to Jupiter?" I asked. "Can *I* take him there?"

I'd never been to space before. It had always seemed exciting—and also really scary.

But nothing was scarier than losing Cosmo. I'd take all the extra time with him that I could get.

"It wouldn't be safe for you to go," Grandma Sadie said. "We don't have space suits in your size."

"Can we sneak out of here and go to the space suit store and buy one?" I asked.

"Space suits cost between three hundred and five hundred million dollars to develop and make," Grandma Sadie said.

I felt my eyes grow wide. Five hundred *million* dollars. I get two dollars for my allowance every week. It'd take me way too long to save up that much.

"Maybe she can borrow a space suit," Claire said.

"I can wear yours, Grandma."

"I'm afraid space suits need to be exactly the right size," Grandma Sadie said. "Mine would be too big on you. And since we haven't sent any kids to space, we don't have one that would work. But don't worry. There are two very experienced AstroBlast explorers going on a mission today in..." Grandma Sadie looked at her watch. "T-minus thirty-two minutes to liftoff."

"Why do they say 'T-minus' when they do countdowns?" Claire asked.

"T stands for the amount of time until the event," Eric explained. "When T is at zero, it's go time."

"So we'd better leave right now," Grandma Sadie said. "Okay, Piper?"

I looked at Cosmo. I only had thirty-two minutes left. Then I'd miss him for the rest of my life!

"Okay," I said.

There was a little secret part of me that hoped we wouldn't make it to AstroBlast in time. I knew it was best for Cosmo if we *did* make it, but I didn't want to say goodbye.

"How will we get out of here?" Claire asked. "Won't the MaLa people be looking for us upstairs?"

"They sure will," Grandma Sadie said. "But in addition to a secret entrance, I also have a secret exit."

Grandma Sadie opened the cabinet under the Bunsen burner. On the outside, it looked like a regular cabinet. But inside, it was a tunnel.

Before today, I hadn't been in any secret passageways. Now I was about to go into my third! If I hadn't been so sad and worried about Cosmo, I would have been excited about it.

This passageway was small. We had to crawl. Grandma Sadie bent down to go first.

Then there was a buzzing sound.

"What's that?" Eric asked.

"Just my phone," Claire said.

"Don't—" Grandma Sadie started.

But it was too late. She'd already answered it.

"Hi, Mom," Claire said. "Oh, hi, Dad. It's both of you. Hey everyone, you're on a video call with my mom and dad."

"Where on earth are you?" Claire's mom asked. "We've been worried sick!"

"I'm in a secret lab at Piper's grandmother's house," Claire said.

I elbowed her in the side.

"Ow!"

"Piper Maclane is with you?" Claire's dad asked.

"Yep," Claire said. "See?"

She held up her phone so I was on camera, too.

"Piper, your parents are also worried sick," Claire's mom said.

"Tell them I'm okay," I said.

"I'll call you later," Claire told her parents. "We have to go to AstroBlast head—"

I reached out and pressed the button to disconnect the call.

"Hey! Why'd you do that?" Claire asked.

"They're safer if they don't know what we're doing, because then the bad MaLa folks won't go after them," I said.

"They're my parents," Claire said. "I'm sure they'll be careful, and we can trust them."

"That's what you thought about your Uncle Ricky," I reminded her.

"I'm sorry," Claire said.

"You don't have to apologize. You trusted someone. There's nothing wrong with that. It's the sign of a good person," I said.

We had reached the end of the tunnel. A tiny door opened, and we were outside of a garage in the middle of the woods. You could barely see Grandma's place from there.

Grandma took out her shoe key, this time placing it into the trunk of a tree. The garage door slowly lifted. Inside, there were a bunch of tarps like the one Grandma had helped us put over the plastic shopping cart.

With a dramatic sweeping motion, Grandma Sadie pulled off one of the tarps. Underneath there were two supercool motorcycles with little sidecars!

"No more shopping carts for us!" she said. "Helmets are on the wall. Grab one. It's T-minus twenty minutes to liftoff. We need to hurry."

"What you *really* need to do," came a voice from behind us, "is hand over that space dust and that slime." We turned to see Doreen and Uncle Ricky blocking our path.

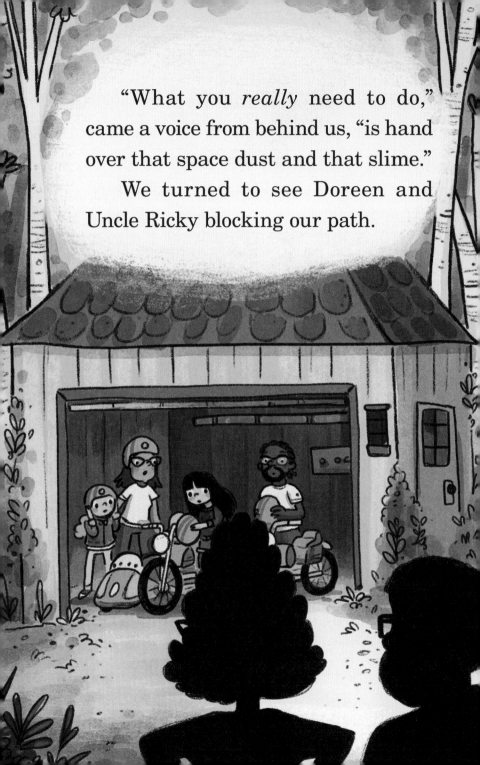

11

JUST PLAY ALONG

"How did you find us?" asked Grandma Sadie.

Doreen laughed. "It was so simple. There's a tracker on that little girl's phone. She's on the same family plan as Ricky."

Uncle Ricky looked at the ground.

Claire's face turned red with anger. "He's not my family! He locked me and my friends up! He lied! He used our secret family knock for evil! I don't have an uncle anymore."

"Claire, I'm so sorr—" Uncle Ricky started.

But Doreen was quick to cut him off. "Enough, Ricky! Hand over the slime and the space dust!"

I had an idea.

I dug into my pocket and pulled out... a bottle of glitter.

"It was never in the slime. That was just a camera trick. Here it is."

Most people probably wouldn't have a bottle of glitter in their pocket, but I'm an artist. An artist always

has supplies with her. You never know when inspiration will strike and you'll need to make art.

(And you also never know when your friend's uncle is going to lock you up and then chase you.)

Glitter comes in all colors. This glitter was silver and gold. Space dust looks exactly like Earth dust—kind of gray and kind of brown and not at all interesting. Nobody believed me when I tried to give them ordinary, dull Earth dust. I hoped Uncle Ricky would believe that sparkly dust was more . . . space-like.

With a shaky arm, I held out the bottle of glitter.

"Noooo!" Grandma Sadie cried. "Piper! You can't do that! You can't give it to them!"

She had tears in her eyes. I wanted to tell her that she had nothing to worry about. But of course, I couldn't tell her, because then Uncle Ricky would hear, and that would ruin everything.

I felt tears prick my eyes, too. I hated upsetting Grandma Sadie.

But then she winked at me.

She winked! That meant she knew exactly what I was doing.

I should have known. Grandma Sadie had seen real-life gray-and-brown space dust. She was just playing along about the glitter. The tears were an excellent touch. She was a really good actress.

"Noooo!" she cried again.

"Quiet!" Doreen said.

She snatched the glitter container out of my hands.

"Yes! This is more like it!" She grinned. "Ricky, examine this! You're our space dust expert," she said, holding it up to Uncle Ricky.

Uncle Ricky had an expression

that I couldn't quite read.

Finally he said, "That's some of the best space dust I've ever seen."

Phew! They bought it!

But out of the corner of my eye I noticed two odd things: Cosmo was staying alive, AND he was more yellow than green.

"Wonderful! I'll take this back to the lab, and you get the blob, in case the girl is lying. Take one of those motorcycles. AstroBlast owes us for causing all this trouble when they should have just given us the space dust in the first place," Doreen said.

Then she stalked off to her car and drove away.

"T-minus eight minutes," Eric said.

131

"Till what?" Uncle Ricky asked.

"Cosmo, that's my pet slime, is very, very sick, and we have eight minutes to get him onto a spaceship headed for Jupiter. It's his only chance," I said.

"Get Cosmo to that launch before Doreen figures out that I just gave her a bottle of glitter and not space dust," Uncle Ricky said.

"Huh?" I said, thoroughly confused. "You knew it was glitter?"

"I used to be a crafter, too," Uncle Ricky said with a small smile. "That was some quick thinking, Piper. Claire, you've picked a good friend."

Claire crossed her arms and turned her head away from her uncle.

"I'm not talking to you," she said.

"I made a mistake," Uncle Ricky said. "A big one. Huge. Gargantuan. I thought getting the dust was the most important thing. But of course, it's not." He turned to Claire. "The most important thing is family," he said. "I'm going to the police to tell them everything and give them the proof that MaLa has been up to some shady stuff lately. I'll get in trouble, but it's the right thing to do."

Uncle Ricky looked sad, but then his expression changed. "Whoa, that slime really *is* alive! Hi, little guy."

My sweet Cosmo had come alive for Uncle Ricky. Cosmo knew he was a good guy, deep down. Claire looked

at Cosmo, then looked at me. She
knew what it meant, too.

"I'm sorry that for a while I forgot
how important family is," Uncle
Ricky said. "But that special secret
knock on the door made me remember
how much I love my brother and my
niece. I'm so sorry about today. I don't
know if I'll ever forgive myself for
what I've done," Uncle Ricky said.

Claire uncrossed her arms and
hugged her uncle.

"You should forgive yourself," Claire said. "I forgive you. Besides, a lot of cool things happened today. I got to rescue someone, then get captured myself, then break out, then go bowling with dominoes, then ride a giant slide, then race in a shopping cart, and then eat astronaut food in a...a secret place."

"And you're about to see a space launch!" Grandma Sadie said. "But we have to hurry!"

LIFTOFF

I was riding in the sidecar of Grandma's motorcycle, and Cosmo— the greatest pet in the world—was in the lunch bag in my lap. Eric and Claire were right behind us.

Cosmo was about to leave me to go to where the space dust was from.

He was headed all the way to Jupiter.

I could see the launchpad out in the middle of a huge field. The shuttle's engines were already revving up and making so much noise. Were we too late?

Grandma Sadie shouted to be heard over the engines. "Okay, this is as far as we can go on the bikes."

"The shuttle is still so far away," I shouted.

"It's not safe to get too close during liftoff," Grandma Sadie shouted back.

I couldn't help crying. I felt tears tracing crooked paths down my cheeks. Cosmo lifted a tiny arm and wiped the tears away.

"TWO MINUTES!" Eric called.

Part of me wanted to miss the shuttle. Then Cosmo would stay with me forever. But I knew I had to be tough.

"Oh, you're the sweetest pet in the whole world," I said. "I'm going to miss you *soooo* much! I miss you *already*!"

A man in an AstroBlast Explorers uniform came rushing toward us in a golf cart. "What are you doing here? It's one minute and forty-two seconds to liftoff! You need to clear the area immediately!"

"I'm sorry, Neal," Grandma Sadie said. "We had a bit of an emergency."

"Oh, Sadie. I didn't realize it was you."

"We need to deliver something to the astronauts on board. It must get to Jupiter as quickly as possible," Grandma Sadie said.

Neal looked at his watch. The seconds to liftoff were ticking by. "One minute and eighteen seconds," he said. "I wouldn't do this for anyone

else. You get off the tarmac. I'll deliver it."

"All right," Grandma Sadie said. She turned to me with her arms outstretched. "Piper," she said.

With Neal there, Cosmo was just a slime blob. Could he hear me in his blob state? I didn't think so, but I wasn't sure.

I couldn't stop crying.

I gave Cosmo a little hug. I knew I wasn't supposed to, but I did. The most love-filled hug I've ever given in my life. I didn't want to say goodbye, but I knew that he was alive because of the space dust, and the space dust belonged on Jupiter.

I felt relieved for Cosmo. I felt sad

141

for myself. And I felt angry at Earth for having the wrong kind of gravity.

It's funny how you can hold all different feelings inside you, all at the same time.

With one last squeeze I whispered, "Goodbye, Cosmo. You'll always be my best friend."

Grandma Sadie took him gently from my arms and handed him over to Neal.

My heart was broken.

Grandma Sadie led us all to the observation room. Maybe I should have been excited to be watching a launch, but all I could think about was Cosmo. We walked up some stairs and into a room. I was barely paying attention. I may as well have been sleepwalking.

Claire exclaimed over everything. "Look at all these windows! They're the biggest windows I've ever seen! And wow—that must be the countdown clock!"

"It is," Grandma Sadie said.

"Fourteen seconds to go," Claire said. "Now thirteen. Twelve. Eleven."

Only eleven seconds until Cosmo

leaves Earth and we're not even on the same planet anymore, I thought to myself.

Eric joined Claire in the countdown.

"Ten... nine... eight... seven... six..."

Grandma Sadie put an arm around my shoulders and started counting down, too.

"Five... four... three... two... one... LIFTOFF!"

There was a blast of smoke from the bottom of the rocket, and the engines fired with a roar so big and so strong that the whole room shook. For a few seconds, all we could see was smoke. But then it started to clear, and we saw the rocket lifting up and up and up. There were golden flames shooting out of the bottom. It went faster and faster, and the room erupted in cheers.

"Wowee!" Claire cried. "Look at it go! I've never seen anything move so fast in my entire life!"

"Space shuttles can accelerate by almost 4,000 miles per hour every minute during the first eight minutes after the launch," Grandma Sadie said.

"No wonder I can't see it anymore," Claire said.

Claire, Eric, and Grandma Sadie all looked at me, excited smiles fading as they remembered why we

were watching the launch and why I wasn't cheering.

"Cosmo is so far away," I said softly.

"You did the right thing, Piper," Grandma Sadie said softly. "Come on, girls. Let's get you two home."

HOME AGAIN

Grandma Sadie drove me home.
Mom and Dad were really happy
when we walked in the door. They
hugged me super hard.

But when they let go, they looked
really, REALLY mad.

"Piper, you know better than to
leave this house without permission

and without telling us where you're going," Mom said. "Your dad and I have been worried sick!"

"We sure have," Dad said. "Now it's straight to your room, young lady. We'll discuss your punishment later."

"It's my fault. I'm too tired to explain right now. It's been a long day," Grandma Sadie told Dad. "Just trust me when I say Piper doesn't need more punishment today."

"Mother, what in the world is going on?"

"Nothing in this world, honey. Nothing in this world," Grandma Sadie said, plopping into the armchair.

"That's all right," I said. "I'm

149

ready to go to bed anyway."

But before I could finish my sentence, Grandma fell asleep sitting up in the armchair.

My mother sighed. "Okay. But I want it all explained tomorrow! Help me with this, Piper."

Mom and I gently covered

Grandma Sadie with a blanket she had crocheted, and Dad gave me a kiss on the head.

"Now off to sleep," he said.

I climbed into bed and pulled the covers over my head. Then I started wondering about things. Things like:

- **What was Cosmo doing right now?**
- **Was he feeling any better as he got closer to Jupiter?**
- **Did he miss me?**
- **Would I ever see him again?**

All these questions swirled around inside my head like planets orbiting the sun as I fell into a deep sleep.

I must have slept and slept. And then...I heard some gurgling.

I could tell it was morning because light from the window was coming in through my eyelids. I didn't open my eyes. I knew I had to be dreaming and I didn't want the dream to end, because Cosmo was in it.

But this dream seemed awfully real. My heart started thump-thumping as hard as it had when Doreen and Uncle Ricky were chasing us.

What if it WAS Cosmo? But what if it WASN'T?

Maybe if I opened one eye, just a smidge, I could find out without spoiling the dream.

I opened my right eye the teeniest of teeny amounts.

And there, sitting on top of the covers, was the cutest, cuddliest, greatest pet in the entire universe.

"Cosmo!" I cried. "What are—"

But then I lowered my voice. Better not wake Mom and Dad. If they came in and Cosmo turned into a slime blob, they'd think I was making slime in my room again. I'm not allowed to do that. I'd get into more trouble, and they might even take Cosmo-the-blob away.

Or maybe he'd finally stay alive for them now that he wasn't as shy.

Now that he was back, I wasn't going to let him out of my sight ever again. I pulled him into my arms and started to hug him tightly. But then I remembered, so I just gave him a gentle little squeeze.

"I don't want to hurt you," I whispered. "I just missed you so much! Come on, let's tell Grandma Sadie that you're here!"

I held Cosmo in my arms and crept down the hall toward the living room armchair.

"Pipsqueak?" Grandma Sadie called. "Is that you?"

I turned toward her voice. She was sitting at the kitchen table, drinking a cup of tea.

"I was just about to wake you. Look who's here!" I said, holding

Cosmo out toward her with a huge smile on my face.

Grandma Sadie also smiled, but it was a knowing smile. "I see you found your little friend."

"You knew he came back?" I asked. "All the way from Jupiter?"

"My astronaut friends said he started to glow right after takeoff. Then he started to shake. And then, poof! He disappeared! I think we just found another one of his superpowers. I won't know for sure until I check him out in my lab, but he looks a happy, healthy purple to me. I'd say he might be back to normal!"

"But won't he get sick again?" I asked.

Grandma Sadie said, "I have a theory."

"What's that?" I asked.

"Give him a hug," she told me.

I hugged him gently.

"Squeeze harder," Grandma Sadie said.

I squeezed a teeny bit harder.

"Give him a real hug," she told me.

I gave Cosmo a real hug, close and cozy and not too tight, but just right. Just like I used to do, before he got sick. He gurgled in my arms. When I looked down at him, he was as purple as ever. His eyes were wide, his cheeks were rosy. He looked just like his old healthy self.

"So...he's better now?" I asked Grandma Sadie. "How did that happen?"

"I noticed that his color started to return when you gave him a really big hug right before he got on the ship. Cosmo is a creature built from imagination, kindness, and love," Grandma Sadie said. "Sure, there's a little bit of space dust mixed in. But

I believe that most of what makes him special comes from you. Your hugs are strong enough to match the gravitational pull of Jupiter."

"So he started to get sick when we were separated, and then I stopped giving him real hugs because I was afraid it would hurt him. I was so wrong!" I said.

I looked down at Cosmo. "Poor little guy," I said. "You were probably scared I'd stopped hugging you forever. But I would never do that. I promise."

Cosmo gurgled happily. We hugged some more.

There was a knock on the door. A knock I recognized.

It went tap . . . tap . . . TAP-TAP-TAP.

My smile couldn't have been any bigger. I ran to let Claire in.

THINGS YOU GET BACK

I tucked Cosmo under my arm like a little slime football and jogged to the door.

"Let's surprise her, Cosmo!" I said. He gurgled happily, and I held him behind my back. Grandma Sadie's face broke into a smile. She shook her head and pulled open the door.

Claire walked in with a somber face.

"I wanted to check in and see how you're doing without—" Claire started, but then I held out Cosmo and she cut herself off. "OMGHU!" she said.

"Huh?" I asked.

"Oh my goodness, hold up," she said. "You made a *new* Cosmo? I thought you didn't have any space dust left!"

"I don't have any left," I said. "This is the same old wonderful Cosmo."

"I don't understand," Claire said. "The space shuttle took off for Jupiter.

I saw it happen."

"Come in, come in," Grandma Sadie said. "We'll explain everything."

"What should I do with my scooter?" Claire asked.

"You got it back?" I asked.

"I don't know how, but Uncle Ricky got it back from MaLa before he went to the police," she said. "He

163

dropped it off with a super sweet note."

"You can leave your scooter right here in the front hall," Grandma Sadie said. She opened the door wider so Claire could come inside.

"He says he changed the wheels, so it should be even faster! Want to take a ride on it today?" Claire asked.

"We'd love that, wouldn't we, boy?" I said.

Cosmo gurgled and nodded his little purple slime head.

There were footsteps behind us. "Piper, Mother," Mom said, still in her sleep shirt. "I'm ready to hear this strange story of yours. Oh...Claire. Piper, you know you have to ask before you invite friends over this early."

I turned around. "I didn't—" I started.

"Whoa!" Mom's eyes grew to twice their normal size.

I looked down at Cosmo, cozily lying in the crook of my arm. He blinked his eyes.

"Well, what do you know," Grandma Sadie said. "He stayed alive. Looks like our little friend here is getting a bit bolder."

Dad walked into the room holding his morning coffee, but he quickly went from holding it to wearing it.

"Ack!" Dad jumped back, spilling coffee all over his pajamas.

Cosmo gurgled, and Dad's mouth fell open.

"Mom, Dad, this is Cosmo," I said. "Cosmo, this is my mom and dad."

They didn't say anything. They just kept staring.

"Let me make some more coffee," Grandma Sadie said. "Tom, Erin, you two sit down. Piper, Claire, Cosmo, and I will explain everything."

Then I gave Cosmo a big hug . . . and he hugged me, too!

My Pet Slime

More to Explore

How Can a Glass Help You Hear Through Walls?

Right now you have a great piece of spy equipment in your kitchen: a drinking glass! Grandma Sadie showed the girls how to hold a glass to the wall to hear Eric in the next room. Because a glass acts like a funnel, it gathers up the vibrations caused by sound waves into a smaller area. When you press your ear against the glass, the sound is amplified. You can try this at home—just make sure the rim of the glass is against the wall and, of course, the glass is empty!

Make an Origami Paper Cup!

1. Get a square piece of paper. If you only have rectangle-shaped paper, cut it into a square.

2. Fold the paper in half by bringing the bottom corner up to the top corner.

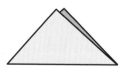

3. Bring the top corner down toward the fold

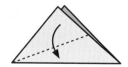

172

so that the edges meet. Press down. Unfold it. You should see a nice diagonal crease line.

4. Fold the left corner to the end of the crease.

5. Fold the right corner to the upper left corner of the folded flap.

6. You should have two flaps of paper at the top. Fold the front flap down.

7. Turn the paper over. Fold the other flap down.

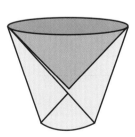

8. Open the pocket. You have a cup!

Meet Sally Ride

Grandma Sadie's inspiration wall includes a photo of Sally Ride, the first American woman in space.

Born in 1951, Sally was always interested in science and math. She earned degrees in physics before training to be an astronaut, and in 1983 she made history when she went on a space shuttle mission. Part of her job was to control the shuttle's robotic arm!

Sally Ride is also the first known LGBTQ astronaut. After going on two space missions and leaving

NASA, Sally Ride wrote several books and created programs to encourage kids, especially girls, to study science and space. She died in 2012. After Sally Ride, many more American women—and women from all over the world—have traveled to space.

SpaceX
Takes Off

It's an exciting and sad moment when Piper watches a rocket blast off with Cosmo inside. On May 30, 2020, Americans watched a real-life spacecraft launch from Kennedy Space Center in Florida. Known as the Crew Dragon, its blastoff marked the first time the United States launched its own astronauts into space since 2011.

A private company, SpaceX, worked with NASA, a government

agency, to make the mission happen. The rocket is also notable because it was developed with technology that allows the rocket to be reused. On May 31, 2020, the two astronauts, Bob Behnken and Doug Hurley, arrived at the International Space Station, where they conducted research and performed tests before returning home.

About the Authors

Courtney Sheinmel is a chocolate lover, a mac-and-cheese expert, and the author of over twenty highly celebrated books for kids and teens, including the middle grade series The Kindness Club, and the young readers' series Stella Batts and Magic on the Map. She lives in New York City.

Colleen AF Venable is the author of the National Book Award–longlisted *Kiss Number 8,* a graphic novel co-created with Ellen T. Crenshaw. Her other books include *Mervin the Sloth Is About to Do the Best Thing in the World* with Ruth Chan, *The Oboe Goes Boom Boom Boom* with Lian Cho, and the Guinea Pig, Pet Shop Private Eye series, illustrated by Stephanie Yue and nominated for the Eisner Award for Best Publication for Kids.

About the Illustrator

Renée Kurilla has illustrated many books for kids. She lives just south of Boston with her husband, daughter, and a plump orange cat who springs to life the moment everyone else falls asleep. Renée loves drawing nature, animals, and projects that require a bit of research. When she is not drawing, she is likely to be found plucking at her ukulele or gluing together tiny dollhouse miniatures.

My Pet Slime:
Saving Cosmo

Andrews McMeel Publishing
a division of Andrews McMeel Universal
1130 Walnut Street, Kansas City, Missouri 64106

www.andrewsmcmeel.com

Epic! Creations, Inc.
702 Marshall Street, Suite 280,
Redwood City, California 94063

www.getepic.com

21 22 23 24 25 SDB 10 9 8 7 6 5 4 3 2 1

ISBN: 978-1-5248-6473-6

Library of Congress Control Number: 2020945167

Design by Carolyn Bahar

Photo credits: page 171, Goryuchkina Yuliya/Shutterstock.com
page 175, Alan C. Heison/Shutterstock.com
page 177, NASA/Joel Kowsky

Made by:
King Yip (Dongguan) Printing & Packaging Factory Ltd.
Address and location of manufacturer:
Daning Administrative District, Humen Town
Dongguan Guangdong, China 523930
1st Printing – 1/4/21

ATTENTION: SCHOOLS AND BUSINESSES
Andrews McMeel books are available at quantity
discounts with bulk purchase for educational, business,
or sales promotional use. For information, please
e-mail the Andrews McMeel Publishing Special Sales
Department: specialsales@amuniversal.com